AN ETERNAL LOVE

By Odayne Marshall

For Vans. Who has stuck by me and encouraged me to keep on going. Always and forever.

CHAPTER ONE

"Hi," I initiated. "Hey," she smiled back. "What's so funny? Please if you may, share the joke." "Oh it's just this lizard; everyone is running away from it." "But you're not. Someone's being brave, I like that" I flirted. The church choir was just about fifteen feet away from us and we watched them in amazement as they prepared in their dutiful practice sessions.

"They sound extremely awesome," I observed. "Not to mention the first elder's wife," she added. "Yes, I agree. Speaking of which, that concert that they are prepping for, I've got tickets for it." "That's very lovely, I'm not sure if I'll be attending as yet. I've got school the following day." "Which school do you attend?" The questions kept popping automatically. "Mega College University" she blushed as she told me what her line of study was.

I couldn't help but noticed how beautiful she was and her smile was as radiant as the scintillating sunshine. It was at this moment that I became sure of her being my most favourite teacher, for she educated me on Richard Valley which is more popularly known as Bamboo Valley and this stroked me surprisingly. I began to ponder, "so if the correct name is Richard Valley, why does everyone call it Bamboo Valley?" it appears to be a mystery I'm yet to unravel.

I too am a member of the men's choral. In fact, we had just sung earlier that same day. I wore a red polyester jacket which illustrated designs of that of an army somewhat. My pants were black and very neatly seamed to match my polished gentleman shoes, finishing off with my most eloquent red and white tie and white shirt. Church was dismissed and everyone was heading out and it was at that particular time I stopped her in her tracks. "Tracey," I beckoned. "Let me have your number," I compelled her. "You'd have to ask my mom" she responded. "Okay" I said as I watched her walk away.

I then headed back inside the church to collect a few things before leaving. Like a flash I rushed as quickly as my feet allowed me to. I intended to ask her mom for her number that same day, I just couldn't allow another week to go by and I didn't. I must admit though, I was impressed. I thought I'd have her number by now but what she did made me respect her even more. I smiled as I hasten out on the road to find her.

I reached at a two-way path and I allowed the Holy Spirit to guide my feet. I quickly spotted her and her mom who greats me warmly. Her mom was very kind to me, she wore a white dress and I think I know the reason to that. Surely to resemble her personality of course and by my estimate she must have been in her thirties for she looked so young and elegant.

We spoke for a minute after which I asked for Tracey's number. However, her mom didn't know it so she beckoned that we walked over to Tracey to get it. On our way over she enquired as to why Tracey's specifically. My smiling made her smiled, "I like her" I blushed. We reached over to Tracey and I was pretty sure she heard when I said that I like her. She spun around smiling with her eyes as they drank from the moonlight. "Yes?" She answered. "He'd like your number" "876..." She began, I handed the phone over to her grasp. "876" she repeated and we bid our farewells after I received it.

Now this was not the first time we saw or spoke with each other. It all started at the tent where we got baptized as a result of the keys to happiness crusade. I made sure to sit with her and from that moment it all began.

I felt a static in my chest, burning with sensation. One that was eager to lit my heart on fire. Not the type that would do damage but the type that would bring warmth, comfort and compassion. Though it was much more than just chemistry. The air froze, the environmental sounds muted and in that moment, at that particular time I knew I was in love with her and as we shared hymnal together I knew she was the one.

They were having wedding anniversary celebration and asked all the celebrating couples to stand. "We should stand" I instructed. She responded with a smile. From then I went and made friends with her mom. Occasionally when the Sabbath ended I would walk with her family to the supermarket, not to purchase anything of my own but to develop a closeness, a bond with Tracey and her family.

Her mom and I would walk and converse on just about anything. It was as if we knew each other for a decade or more. We spoke on my career, spirituality, church, family and I learnt that she had known my grandmother who was now deceased. In fact, they were great friends. It was one of those evenings while walking with her that I learnt that Tracey's sisters were twins. I couldn't have told just by looking, they weren't the identical type. I told her that Tracey has her resemblance which she took as a compliment.

One of Tracey's sisters was taller than the other; she had a great speaking voice. One that deserves to be in any movie. She was of light complexion and always wore her hair in a modest and classy manner. She wasn't afraid to speak up and make her point. In fact, she does this with confidence and certainty. Her name was Marvette. Marvette and I had been asked to participate in the conduct of Sabbath school by our Elder. She had the scripture reading and I the prayer. We did exceptionally well as expected by our peers and especially because Tracey was looking on. There she was sitting with her younger sister Maria by her side. Maria was usually cheerful and was twin to Marvette.

The following morning while making my way to work I've managed to take the time out to send Tracey a message. "Good morning Tracey. It was very nice seeing you yesterday" it read. To my astonishment, she replied. "Good morning Nardo. It was very nice seeing you yesterday too." With this I was certain my day would be marvellous. We didn't speak much that first week, yet I anticipated Sabbath to arrive so I could see her again.

It was getting close to the day of the concert as we woke up that morning with much to discuss. It was the phase two people that's interested in each other journey on when escalating fondness of friendship. There wasn't a day that went by where we did not speak to each other; as a matter of fact we spoke all day every day to be precise. There was a certain feeling in the air. If I could just use one word to describe it, I'd say it was euphoric. We have both established how we felt for each other and what we wanted to do; to be together.

It came to a very important day for both of us. December 17, 2016, I had a question I needed to ask of her. It was one that would be life changing and I was eager to do so, I arrived at church early for once. We didn't sit together but I noticed her checking me out, yes that was because I was doing it too of course. I smiled and waved at her and she did likewise. I knew she was going to say yes. I was certain. The thing is I'm always good at reading body languages and auguries.

After the Sabbath ended I walked with her where we arrived at our destination which was close to Bamboo Valley. There we were standing facing each other with my favour at the tip of my tongue. "Will you..." I started, "be my girlfriend?" I proposed. "...Yes" she accepted congruently. We then made it known to our families of our decision. They were just as excited as we were.

It was time for work and I made it to work safely. The thing is I'm not very good at multitasking and Tracey had something very important to discuss in person. I had a feeling it wasn't something good. We got to church. She was on the platform along with her sister Maria. Then it happened. I've been trying my very best to be cheerful and happy but as it turned out I was only pretending.

The truth is I was feeling morose. We sat directly facing each other, which I didn't think was coincidental. Our eyes met and I couldn't hide how I felt any longer, she knew. After the service I made my way over to her and greeted her with a handshake and we spoke. I knew what was coming; it was the cessation of us. I didn't want that to happen at all. I tried to walk away before she could say it but she stopped me in my tracks.

Maybe I was being tenacious but it hurts very much. I went through the whole day with a brick in my windshield. The evening's activities were extremely fun, yet I felt ripped off. It was filled with items of songs and a humorous skit which made me laugh, but still there was something missing. There was someone missing. Tracey wasn't there. She had made it known to me from earlier that she wouldn't return so I did not spend the evening section with her. Like the others, I too had an item to showcase, a poem. Which I delivered fluently and received comments that motivated me in respective of who it came from. During all this excitement and fun, I couldn't keep my mind focused on what was happening around me long enough. I'd occasionally zone out to day dream of her, of Tracey.

I kept thinking to myself that it didn't make any sense. Why allow me to find her that evening when I arrived at the two-way path? Why allowed us to develop this bond of closeness if it was never going to work out? Then it hit me, it's not a break up at all. I wasn't sure where my theory originated from but it kept me grounded and smiling. I noticed I've been receiving messages from her while I was still in church so I replied back as soon as I got home.

Be as it may I wasn't the only one going through pain. I could see where she wanted to continue our relationship and I was determined to give her more attention. So there we were back on our feet again, just like that. We were elated and it could be that it was the season of a happy holiday. Her birthday had just passed recently. It was while we were friends, only just a few days before we got together. I wished her a happy birthday and we spent the holiday together. We had a date planned in January. We were to go get ice cream at the mall and have a walk through the park. However, as amazing and romantic it sounds, it got postponed until a later date.

CHAPTER TWO

I t was the 15th of January, a Sunday and we went to church in the night. Tracey'sschool resumed the following day and she had to get preparing. I made it my utmost priority to walk her home that night; I needed to be sure she was safe. "How are you?" I started. "Good night Nardo. I'm good, thanks and you?" "Good evening Trace, likewise."

I've given her a nickname. One that was originated by and had a co-founder of yours truly, me. It was a variation of her Christian name and also a brand name. She was curious to know why that name, so I told her that she is a name brand to me. I told her that she's eminent. Yes, it was sweet to say which she liked very much but I also meant it. Which I'm sure she adores and appreciated even more.

As we walked together I enquired on the proceedings of her preparations. "Are you ready for school tomorrow?" I asked suavely." "No" she responded quickly. "Why? Isn't school fun?" I chuckled a bit. "No, it's too much stress." We arrived at her stop and bid our farewells.

The following day she journeyed to Mega College University and we text of having a movie night together. Just the two of us, after all we deserved it. School was dismissed and she didn't quite get a bus to take her all the way home, only partially. I offered to come get her and immediately got ready to hit the road. I didn't have a car of my own or neither someone I could think of that would readily be prepared to hit the road like I am to go get her.

The night was late and I needed to get Trace home. I knew I wasn't going to get a cab or bus to take me where she was at this time so I decided to charter a cab. Though it was a charter it had to be a driver I'm very familiar with on a day to day basis. I paved the street with my feet and quickly found a cab that was interested in accepting the task ahead. However, the driver had a change of mind and went home due to the time of the night. I was on the road still determined to get another and I didn't get another as quickly as the first but eventually I did. Instantly I told Trace and she was elated. This driver though made a trip that was five minutes to Garden District which I allowed. He might have taken ten minutes but he came back and we headed to get Trace. She was close so we had to drive very quickly.

We made it in record time though she was waiting a while just the same. She then made it known to me that her mom and sisters were on their way also so I made the cab go back without us while I waited with her. I was so happy to see her. It was the first time I ever saw her in her uniform and she looked amazing. She wore a sweater over her uniform which had an auburn colour with the reflection of the street lights. Over her hand she held her umbrella which appealed classy in my sight and her backpack neatly caresses her back. I had brought my sweater for I saw that the night was a bit chilly and the sweater could come in quite handy. However, it wasn't for me but for Trace.

There we stand in the middle of the street as we waited patiently. "I'd like to read you something" I said. "Okay." She responded. "If all the world and love were young, and truth in every shepherd's tongue, these pretty pleasures might me move, to live with thee and be thy love. But could youth last and love still breed, had joys no date nor age no need, then these delights my mind might move, to live with thee and be thy love." "What is that?" She curiously enquired. "It's a poem" I answered. "I like it."

At this point I could feel her body moving closer to mine and there was a mutual feeling in our hearts. She felt it too, I'm sure. I placed my right hand on her shoulder which stretched over her back. Then lowering down to her biceps. She had her arms folded across her chest and then softly she met mine as we clasped together. "Thanks for coming" she began. "It means a lot to me." "Your welcome, I wouldn't leave you all alone in this solitary place." We smiled together.

We then saw a car approaching and it appeared to be Tracey's family. We went right across as soon as the car came to a halt. Her mom popped out along with her sisters and they greeted us pleasantly. The car had adequately just about enough room for all of us. Maria got in first, then Trace, followed by me and Marvette. Her mom occupied the front seat next to the driver which was over the age of forty by my estimate.

There was a gas station close by and we made a stop for some gas. Her mom made sure we were all okay and shortly after we were on our way home. There was music playing in the car.

The type that could calibrate any mood on perfect. It was soft, slow music and perfect for romance. It so happened that our hands began touching as it was our reflexes to do so. Softly we aimed, with finger tips against finger tips, then occasionally stirring the middle of her palms. She tugged on my shirt and I turned my head to face her and our eyes met. For a few seconds we held that posture as the atmosphere around us escalated.

I then moved in for the kiss but she pulled away. It happened again; the intensity. This time I told her I love her. "I love you" she whispered with our eyes in contact. We were heading close to our stop by now and we prepared to head out. First Marvette, then myself holding hands with Trace and Maria followed after us. Her mom got out also and we walked in threes and twos with Trace and I at the back. We came to a stop as the three sisters went to see their dad. So her mom and I waited for their return.

"Thanks for coming Nardo. I totally appreciate it very much." "Sure, you're welcome. I know it must be quite hectic traveling to and from school every day." "Yes and Tracey gets up early each morning to do so. She usually goes twice per week last semester but this time around its required that she goes every day." "Well it'll all pay off very soon. I look forward to that happy graduation day." "Indeed." She agreed.

By now Trace and her sisters were heading back to us and we continued in groups of threes and twos. Holding hands, she began, "In case you didn't hear, I said that I loved you." "I love you too" I responded meaningfully. "Did you hear?" "Yes" I confessed. No sooner than I had finished my sentence she pulled her hand away free from mine. I told her that I had said it before her and she reached back for my hand.

While walking I misplaced my step and almost came to a fall but luckily she held on to me. "Be careful" she said. It was from this moment onward that I knew I'd be safe in her arms, just as I intended on keeping her safe. We were approaching to my stop and I had to go. However, neither of us wanted the night to end. It was a beautiful night. One that was filled with love of two hearts becoming one. We hugged and both said goodnight at the same time which was cute. "Okay, let me know when you get home." "You too." Then I watched her as she catches up with her mom and sisters and I got in a cab home.

The following Sabbath morning I visited another church with my family. I had already made it known to Trace from the middle of the week about this and she was okay with it. This church that I visited was called Lakers S.D.A church.

It was much smaller than my membership church but very comfortable. I soon recognized that many of us had visited too so we weren't alone. I remember coming to this church when I was much younger with my grandmother and everything was still the same and quite familiar so I knew my way around. The day was incredible, from Sabbath school to vespers and I learnt a lot especially in Bible study time and Adventist youth. Though the day was great, there was still something missing from the equation; someone missing. I missed her so much and I couldn't wait until I got home to tell her of my day and how much I had missed her. As expected, she had missed me too.

The following day we went to church in the night and there I saw her awaiting me just outside. She wore the most eloquent pink dress I've ever seen in my whole entire life of twenty plus years and counting. She looked beautiful. I greeted her family and went over to say beside her. There we spoke of romance and plans for our future as we softly met finger tips with finger tips again. We sat together during church and when it has dismissed she walked slowly so that I could catch up with her.

"Hi, what's up?" my hand caressed her lower back. "Good evening Nardo. I'm good, thanks. You?" "Likewise. Are you cold?" I softly brushed her triceps with the back of my hand very passionately. "A bit." She responded. I had planned on walking her all the way home. "Coming Nardo?" Our Elder asked. "I'm not quite ready as yet" I answered. "You can go if you like" she offered. "Are you sure?" "Yes." We were at the gate when we bid our farewells. "Okay, goodnight. I love you." "Goodnight, I love you too." We gestured to each other in embrace and then it happened so quickly.

I gave her a kiss on her neck. It was a full kiss, meaningful and romantic. I could tell by the look in her eyes that she didn't expect it but loved it very much. I then watched her as she caught up back with her family. I made my way back to our Elder. "Changed your mind?" He asked. "Yes." I responded, as we journeyed home.

We had made plans that I would ask her mom for her hand in marriage and both were excited. Her bus wasn't coming all the way home again and I wanted to go get her like before. Her family was going so she convinced me that she'd be okay. On Sabbath morning I came to church to see her waiting for me. The music was soothing and the air blissful. I always look forward to Sabbath days for its the best day of the week in my opinion and hers. We get to spend the whole day together. I still had that very important question to pull off. It was one that her mom knew not about for I asked Trace not to tell her of our plans on asking. I wanted to be the one to do it. I think it's better that way. So I made my way over to her mom and we started talking. With her talking always comes easy to me.

"Hi" she scooted over as I sat. "How's it going?" "Great, thanks. I'm just exploring the surroundings" I told her. "Where will the choir be seated?" I asked. "Normally it's up by the front on the platform. Though I don't think there are enough benches for everyone." "It's roughly about twenty of us on the choir." We began counting together an estimate as to how many the benches would accommodate. We came to the conclusion that it would suffice. I told her that I'll be singing come the following week also.

We've been encouraged by our Sabbath school leader to sit in our designated classes so as to decrease the level of haphazard conducts. It was quite wonderful of the placements we've been issued. "Where do young adults normally sit?" I asked. "They normally sit upstairs on the balcony."

I looked over to the area where Trace was and then asked, "how do you feel about Tracey and I being together?" I already knew that she was okay with it but I was going somewhere with the conversation. "Well, Tracey decides on what she wants and she's an adult to choose who she wants to be with so I don't have a problem with it." I then followed up and told her that I'd like to marry Trace very soon and she was happy about it also.

CHAPTER THREE

It was a wonderfully cool evening as we made our way to prayer meeting. We were touched and learnt on a message that was encouraging in trying times and many of us gave testimonies. I listened as they spoke on how good the Lord has been to them and that we should keep strong in the faith of Jesus. I walked with Trace and her family to the gas station, then home.

When we arrived at the gas station there we encountered on numerous vehicles. I instantly remembered that I had told her I'd give her driving lessons soon and so onward I asked. "Which of these cars would you like to take your lessons with?" She looked around and replied "it's not here."

I then noticed her staring at my hymnal so I told her the duration I've had it and we had a friendly and jovial feud on whether it was a long time or not. When we were closing to her gate I took the measurement of her finger and bid our farewells thereafter. By this time, it was approaching unto Valentine's Day and as any other romantic lady I'm sure she was looking forward to it. We didn't speak of it much as to build anticipation for her to see what will happen. Only just two days to go I asked her to be my valentine and as expected she accepted.

On the 14th of February we made sure to wake up early and hit the road. I was dressed for the occasion; red and white shirt, with white shorts and sneakers. I was in such a rush to head out that I forgot to take with me her gift and had to return for them. I did take a few minutes longer than I'd expected but she was also waiting on her bus which didn't arrive as yet. The morning was blissful and the wind was cool and relaxing. There was love in the air. I got her a red rose, a real rose. Maybe it was pink though but that all depends on the eyes of the beholder. I also made her a beautiful card with a poem that I composed and finishing off with a nugget chocolate all placed in a handy gift bag. The poem went something much like this: Princess Trace.

> "I knew that I was in love from the moment I laid sight on her,
> Am I exaggerating?
> Mayhap not.
> Oh the thoughts, the decisions, the persuading, the schemes;
> I had to be sure so I pay close attention,
> Like a cat, I studied my prey,
> I waited patiently yet attentively,
> Just for the perfect moment to make my kill.
> It is a wonder of how miraculously it seemed,
>   That a mere lady of comely appearance could set my mind to flow words such as these,
> Oh her skin so soft and smooth,
> And her lips I'd like to taste,
> If time could spend then we'd be millionaires,
> I like her company and her listening ears.

A love so pure,
A love so kind,
A love so beautiful,
A love so blind.
I am amazed of life's design,

When two people decide to cross the line.
The border of marriage and beyond,
For decades to come we shall sing this song.
I knew that I was in love from the moment I laid sight on her,
Am I exaggerating?
Mayhap not.
I love you Princess Trace,
Always and forever,
Happy Valentine's Day,
My Queen, My Treasure."

She was waiting by the gas station with her mom when I got there. It was the second time seeing her in her school uniform and she looked just as amazing as the first time. We were very excited to see each other and it was blatant on both our faces. I handed her my gift and she thanked me for it. I could tell she wanted to kiss me. Though we didn't, that didn't cause the morning to be any less wonderful. I went home that morning feeling all good inside. It was true love and I could tell.

The following Sabbath was youth's day at church and the youth's choir was prepared to perform. I too had arrangements on the programme which was the offertory and vesper voice. I had matched with Trace for the very first time. She was eloquently put together in her fashionable black heels, smooth white skirt with black flower petals and black blouse to match with her grey jacket which neatly caressed her body. She was beautiful; she wore her hair in an upright and modest manner. It always brings out the beauty in her eyes.

I wore my well-polished gentleman shoes with grey pants with seams of the military and white long sleeved shirt with my grey tie. I also had on my black vest under my grey jacket. Finishing off with the neatest of haircuts and my timepiece on my left wrist. She was elated to see me and I just know by the look in her eyes just how she felt inside. I made quite a scene of laughter while on the podium, good laughter that brings happiness to the congregation; I did well. The evidence was on her face. She was happy and pleased. We had a marvellous day together. It was perfect and we held hands as we walked home together.

We were both excited to go to church the following night; February 19, 2017. We ironed our clothing together even though we lived apart, as it was our custom. This was cute. It was a surprise to me while I walked her home that night to hear her say she had a gift for me. I hadn't expected any as she hoped I'd like it. I made it known unto her that I know I would. "Do not open it until you get home" I heard her say. I was so ecstatic inside and somehow I never did want that moment to come to a cessation. The air around us sprouts a blissful aroma of delightful love at its highest quality. I must have slipped my arms around the small of her back, for I felt her body close against mine in synchronized embracement and affection, followed by a kiss on her neck.

Bidding her a farewell in goodnight, we must have stood there for a while as we didn't want to depart. Still I hastened home so that I could read the card she presented to me. It read:

"To: His Royal Highness Nardo.

From: Trace, with love.

You are my sunshine.

Who is my first thought each morning and the last each night before I lay my head to rest?

Who has allowed me to see just how special I am?

Who has been more patient with me than anyone I know? And has loved me even when I am not sure I am worthy?

Who has given me a new perspective on life?

And, who do I want to spend the rest of my life with?

The answer to all the above questions is you Nardo.

You are my source of happiness. I know I have messed up multiple times but you are the part of my life that I can't live without. I love you. Always and forever. Happy Valentine's Day."

There was something quite overwhelming in emotion about the card as I read each word and just as I knew I'd loved it, I did. I started walking around with a great smile on my face, one would think I'm in love. So we went to bed feeling happy.

On one particular evening while church dismissed I watched her go early, just a few minutes before. I've always adored her walking, for she walked glamorously and classy. Like a magnetic force field, we were bond together; it wasn't a surprise to me that no sooner than I exited the church property I quickly came upon her. "Look, look!" Marvette shouted emphatically. "Yeah, it's Nardo and I can't believe he's here. How'd you find us?" asked Mom and Maria.

The answer was a fond tale that only Trace and I knew of. We were linked magically together. We could feel each other's pulse, we knew what the other was doing even being a distant away and we knew when the other entered the room. But of course I only just gave a smile as my response. Trace most of all was the happiest to see me show up. One would begin to think she had summoned me with her thoughts and as it happened it came through. The sign outside read 'Juicy Patties' when I entered. "Hi, how are you?" I flirted. "I'm good thanks, you?" she smiled back. "I'm great." Trace was in the line purchasing patties for everyone, as she enquired if I required. It was a query in which I accepted, but hesitantly by means of playing with her. I gave my sister Marvette a brochure from church then headed on the road.

We arrived at a very cool seating, the evening air was blissful with the radiance of the sunset in the heavens above us. There was something about this setting, it wasn't a date but it felt like it could have been. We spoke of a mango tree that was right ahead of us. When we were finished eating, I walked her home, holding hands as it was always our custom. We arrived upon a beautiful rose. I didn't recognize it at first but I saw Trace focusing her chakra of meditation on them and I thought how eloquent they were. I pointed out, "those look nice" "yes they do, you got me that one.

I am so sorry, I should have given it to mom to bring home for me, instead of bringing it to school with me because I tried putting it in water but it was too late." "That's okay, there was a reason I didn't get you a fake rose." "Why is that?" She asked. I told her that my love for her isn't fake and it was true, it made perfect sense. It amazes me how time can run so quickly when we are having a good time. We quickly arrived upon our destination and we bid our farewell like I was going away to the war and she wouldn't see me again for quite a while.

The following week I woke up extremely earlier than the usual time. It was a wonderful day, certainly the atmosphere made a promise of it. I quickly made fix so I could be calibrated present at my regular morning routine, which was running. The air was blissful and peace. I could feel a sensation of goodness all over. I did five whopping laps and I could sense the sun making its way out as it greeted me a pleasant good morning. I couldn't keep my mind off Trace, which was one thing for sure. If I'm not sure about anything before, I'm most definitely sure about that. So I picked up the phone as soon as I got home and texted her. Today was a grand day which promises a great night to come; I carefully picked out my outfit for the occasion with the thought in mind that Trace will be attending.

CHAPTER FOUR

I've been appointed a great task at church; which was to present a reading to the congregation. Professionally dressed for the occasion I comfortably attired myself in a sleek black and white outfit; from my belt down to my shoe I wore all black, my shirt was white to balance it out, with my black timepiece on my left wrist. But I just couldn't leave out my black tie; it made so much of a difference. "I love your tie." Or "nice tie" Trace would say. So I made sure I double checked in the mirror I had it on before exiting the house that evening.

I tried to be early for the event of the night so I kept glimpsing over at my timepiece while being in the cab and I hoped the time would just for once be dishonest; I was extremely late I thought. However, upon my arrival as it turned out I wasn't. Everyone else was late also which in turn made me early. I could hear the music playing from a far off. No sooner than I had taken my seat I extolled God in prayer.

There was to be music by the youth's choir of the church. I saw them arraying themselves in order in their designated seating area. More people were now coming in and shortly after it was Trace and her family. She was dressed in the most beautiful pink dress I've ever seen in my whole entire life and I was well pleased at how eloquent she was. We didn't sit together though, her sisters sat with me and Trace sat at the back with mom.

The evening's proceedings got on the way and the night was blessed with heavenly singing of hymns and popular gospel records. The presentations were great too and as it was my custom I delivered my cut to the best of my ability. It was one of those nights we all never want to come to a cessation.

At dismissal everyone wanted to greet me, though I wasn't sure why. When I got outside I saw where Trace was pacing at a slow so that I'd catch up with her I imagined. "Hi, how are you? How'd you enjoy the night?" I enquired. "It was really great, thanks and you?" "It was awesome, thanks." It was at this point that she saw it importantly fit to explain to me why we didn't sit together earlier, which was because mom could use some company at the back. After all, it was her favourite seat.

There was something we both had to share with each other that night; something that was promised to be good. It was late but that didn't stop the multitude of people parading on the street. I pulled her closer to my body as our arms interlace with each other in holding hands, the way a bride and groom would on their wedding day coming down the aisle. This was to assure her that she was safe and secure. By the look on her face, I could tell that it was working. "So" I began. "You had something you'd like to say?" I reminded her, not that I thought she'd forgotten but to prompt her into beginning. "Oh, yes. You first." "Ladies before gentleman." "Adam before Eve." Us men always end up going first when traveling down this road so I went first. While I spoke we both felt elated and a sense of happiness aroused amongst us.

After I've finished we made our way through a tumult where I allowed her to walk ahead for our passage only allowed for single file. Shortly thereafter we were cuddled together again and that was when she told me her bit. It was beautifully said and I appreciated every word of it. We were heading to dad's place. When we were close Trace and her sisters went ahead, while mom waited outside with me by the gas station. Now mom and I was always happy whenever the opportunity pops up for us to have a talk together.

They were gone for a few minutes so we had more than enough time on our hands to discuss my preaching passion, my grandmother and Trace's mom, my little brother taking on examinations to attend a new school, and we even touch on Trace and I. By that time, they were back and we were so happy to see each other. I think I had missed her too in that short period of time.

It was incredible. Our eyes met, her palms in mine and it was a blissful experience. It felt awesome. We were walking for quite a while and as we arrived to our destination, Trace decided to take a week apart from me. This week apart would include no communication at all, no texting, no phone calls and we wouldn't sit together in church. A day apart would have been unbearable and uneasy. I didn't think that it was possible to make a day but we needed to do this. I wished her a goodnight and I soon after arrived home myself.

There I thought to myself, what have I done? How could I let this happen? I completely blamed myself for the whole thing. So I went to bed that night feeling like I've lost a precious diamond jewelry. The following morning, I texted her, well I just had to. I knew it wasn't a week as yet but I found myself messaging her that morning. I was always a bit tenacious when it comes on to her. We had spoken and it has been known unto me that there will be an additional day unto the time apart for it needed to be seven complete days so without further locomotion I acquiesced the request at hand. It's only a few days I told myself.

Tuesday was the hardest because we usually wake up together on those days. I always enjoyed and adored the scintillating sunrise in the mornings. Then came the other day, the week just ran by so quickly; not. I went to church in the middle of the week with her mom and sisters. There her mom and I spoke of this week apart. "How's Trace doing Nardo? Have you heard from her?" I knew mom already knew for Trace had mentioned she'd tell her of it but this was her way of discerning clarification. "We haven't spoken; we are taking a week apart" I managed. "Oh my, so you two haven't spoken since the other night?" She asked, making reference to Sunday night. "Well we spoke on Monday because I had texted her then." I could get the sense of feeling that her mom wasn't very happy about us not communicating so I cheered her up with a photograph. It was a photograph that portraits Trace's engagement ring and wedding band. It must have worked somewhat, for mom dressed herself in her most eloquent of smiles. "So crusade begins on Friday night" I added. "Will you be attending?" She asked. "God's will, yes. How about you?" "I'm not sure about Friday but Saturday is sure."

I quickly remembered Trace and I having a conversation about youth's fellowship on Friday nights. "I don't usually go" she'd say. We prayed together holding hands and when it got close to the cessation of the service, mom told me that she's about to go. It was something they'd normally do. They had to meet Trace when she gets off the bus from school. "Would you like to come?" She enquired. I was silent for a few seconds' tops. Yes! I wanted to shout but I knew it would be best if I didn't instead. "Yes I do, very much but I'll stay. Thanks." "Should I say hi to Trace for you?" "Yes, tell her I... tell her that I miss her a lot." "Okay I will" she replied.

As I watched mom, Marvette and Maria made their way to the exit, I grew a penitent look on my face. It was Friday night, the beginning of the crusade as a high proliferation of people turned out for the night's proceedings. My mom accompanied me.

It was promised to be good and indeed it was. The message which was presented connected to the wide mass of congregation including myself. It was a richly blessed evening and we all went home feeling spiritually filled.

On Sabbath morning I tried to be early for church. There were various reasons for this. Firstly, I was always one who tried my very best to showcase my punctuality whenever an opportunity presented itself at hand. Also I was scheduled to present the scripture reading for Sabbath school that particular morning. But most of all why I rushed so much was to see Trace. There she was sitting on the top floor with her sisters, displaying all the features of a beautiful princess.

Our eyes met in correspondence with each other and immediately, in the twinkling of an eye, we zoned out our surroundings and its particularities thereof. I could sense a feeling of satisfaction; our presence assuaged each other so much that our hearts delighted in a congruent covenant. I went up the stairs to where her highness was and sat beside her as it was our custom.

"Happy Sabbath" I initiated in general. "Happy Sabbath" they all responded. "How's mom?" I focused my attention on Trace. She didn't reply immediately, she waited patiently as a cat would before entering a door like it had all the time in the world to do so. It was as if she didn't hear the question, either that or she's very well at feigning. She then places her index finger on her lips and I could tell she was trying hard not to indulge in a smile. The church usually groups each Sabbath school classes together in sections and we were in the same class. Though we agreed not to sit together, I just had to. I couldn't help it even if I tried. "Nardo, will you be going back downstairs after Sabbath school?" She asked. This was when I placed my index finger on my lips, just as she had done a few minutes ago. This was cute.

Two weeks later we went to Sunday night evangelistic meeting at church, there was a panel discussion on 'the state of the dead' so I prepared myself for it by reading on the topic in the Bible. The evening was cool and chill. I was careful to dress appropriately for the night; I didn't forget my tie. The world was sure to explode had I done that. Upon arrival at the church I whispered a prayer to my God, my heavenly Father. Then came Trace and her family. No sooner had she came through the door, we automatically greeted each other with smiles of joy and a high proliferation of happiness.

The panel discussion was informative and very interesting. We sat very close together. There wasn't any space between; any closer and we'd be on top of each other. The air bloomed bliss and it poured over our heads like showers of blessings. We held hands; mayhap I should say we titillated each other's palm in a motion of satisfaction and joy. That night as I walked Trace home, I got the feeling she was a bit cold so I insisted on keeping her warmer as we made our way to a quick stop at a small retail shop where we purchased a number of items before making our way home to say goodnight with a strong kiss on her neck.

CHAPTER FIVE

The next day Trace made her way to school. One bright and sunny Monday morning, I got up that morning quite early as it was always my custom in doing so, for I just needed to get my exercising routine on the way. After I've completed, I felt refreshed and fully equipped to take on the day ahead. I was expecting a parcel which was to be delivered to me. It was Trace's engagement ring and wedding band. Exceedingly excited I made my way to the post office that afternoon and to my astonishment it was there waiting for me like a puppy waiting for its master. I immediately lost my patience in signing for it. One would think I'm a doctor by profession by the look of my penmanship. Quickly stuffing it in my blue one strap bag on my right shoulder I hastily made my way outside and back home.

The whole time journeying home I wore a prodigious smile on my face; cheek to cheek. No sooner than I had gotten inside the house I typed a text message to Trace to tell of the great news but I didn't send it immediately for I knew she was still in class. The rings were rather dashing and adorable to behold. I practically stared at them the whole day. "Is this what love looks like?" I questioned the mirror. "Yes" the mirror replied, or so I imagined. When Trace's class was over that evening I told her of the great news and by her exclamation she was just as elated as I was, if not more. We spoke a full conversation relating to the topic for the remaining of the day, no exaggeration.

Tuesday night was scheduled for school's challenge quiz and our hometown school made the finals as it was their custom. We were increasingly elated to see the match that it went viral and trending all over the country; it was that prodigious of a play off. However, Trace was unable to make it home before it had begun streaming live. That was when I volunteered to keep her up to date with the scores and the proceedings of the match via short message service.

I poured a nice glass of fruit juice to drink as I prepared myself for the match to begin. Excited would be subtracting from my emotions as the match started. I sipped my juice, whispered a prayer as I was completely confident that we'd win the match for our school appeared infallible and immaculate.

We lead the match throughout the first two rounds of the game but were overtaken by the opponent team. As a result, we became the runner ups that year. I was shocked but I knew that we put up a great fight in the end. After all, someone told me that it's not about winning but about having fun. It was that same night Trace complimented on my perfume from the previous night.

I then went to prayer meeting at church during the course of the week with her mom and two sisters. Trace was absent from church that evening; she was on her way home from school. We had a great service that evening. Much prayer was involved and plenty persons gave their testimonies including Maria. I could tell that it was a very emotional experience for her for that was the first time I have ever seen her cried. I too grew a sense of melancholy, especially because I was so close to her. I was touched and my reflexes prompt me to give her comfort and assurance that it would be okay but unfortunately I froze up. I've always done this, the first time it happened was when I lost my grandmother and I cried on the inside which was very painful. I think I've done this for my mom. She was sad and that was why I needed to be strong.

Upon receiving a text message from Trace, her mom and both sisters decided to leave church a bit early before it was over so that they could meet her. "Nardo, we're going now okay." Mom told me. "I'm coming too" I fixed to get going with them. Now Trace had no idea I plan on paying her a surprise visit per say. At least I didn't inform her on it but she's a brilliant one so I figured she must have known or hinted to it at the very least. "Does Trace know that you're coming along with us Nardo?" Mom asked. "Well I didn't tell her, it's to be a surprise but maybe she does."

We made our way hastily on the streets in conversation. "Last night there was plenty persons in town to see the match." "Did you see it? What do you think about it?" "Well they tried, they had to. They were going so well all the way up to the end and Trace told me you kept her up to date with what's happening while she was on the bus coming home so thank you." "You're welcome." We got to the location where Trace would make her stop. Marvette stood beside me. "You two are at the same height, isn't that so?" Mom proclaimed. "I guess" we all agreed. "You should hide quickly before Trace comes Nardo. Come girls, hide him."

The bus pulled up and I've always had good sight for God has blessed me in that department, I saw a Princess clothed with royalty and beauty emerging and making her appearance. "Hi" we greeted. I've watched her unwrapped her head wrap and shortly after I reached for her hand as we paved the street with two sets of footprints. We walked at the back behind mom and her sisters. I had a really great surprise for her. It was her seeing me; me walking her home but there was something else quite special to it than just that. I had written a small note and I planned on slipping it under her pillow but that wouldn't be possible at this point so I thought, what nice bag she has after seeing her pulling a bottle of water from it to drink. "Let me see your book" I aimed at being compelling. "Why do you want to see my book?" She asked. I didn't expect that question at all. "To see what you did at school today" I managed. "What I did at school today is at school and not in my book." What is it going to take? I thought to myself. We arrived up to our stop; her home and I gave her the note, hugged and wished her a goodnight. It was at that point that she realised what I was trying to do and she texted an apology for being so stubborn. "You wouldn't be Trace if you weren't" I replied. "And you wouldn't be Nardo if you didn't have something sweet to say about it."

The night ended perfect and there isn't anything that I would alter about it. Sunday; April 2, we planned on going to church in the night to evangelistic service. It was a day that grew long and sure as heaven took its measurable time in advancing to a cessation. Now surely that wasn't the only thing I had planned;

I made sure not to leave her engagement ring that evening so I kept checking whether it was in my sweater pocket. Prior to heading out to grab a cab, I made some preparations by practicing what to say, how to say it and going down on one knee but I soon realized that each time I came up with diverse words and phrases so I thought to myself "I got this."

Dressed immaculately for the occasion in a sneaker, dark fitted jean, a yellow shirt that illustrates her name all over 'Trace' to remind us that she's a name brand to me, finishing with my comfy sweater. Though the sweater made the look more sophisticated, the main reason for it was to hide the box of rings in its pocket so she wouldn't see it for I had nowhere else to place it. It was the biggest surprise ever, she knew I intend on proposing but I figured she just didn't know when I would and I guess that was the fun part about it.

Getting close to the time of the service to begin I pulled up at the church a few minutes early, maybe five minutes or so I thought. I don't know but I was lead upstairs by a spiritual force mayhap, even though the service would be kept downstairs. To my surprise, I saw colours of iridescent in a pattern of roses, decorations and I personally felt like the air tasted blissful. There was a long carpet in the center of the room arraying from the top to the back. The chairs were nicely put together and I could see an oval shaped decoration, the size of a man at the top of the alter. By the look of it I could tell that a wedding was held there earlier in the day. It was a green, pink and white wedding, very beautiful to behold. I went up closely and took a seat. There I prayed to God; my heavenly Father.

After which I thought to myself, it's not by chance that I planned on doing this deed tonight and to arrive at church to see this setting before me. I texted Trace instantly to tell her that there's something I'd like her to see. Now I know she was excited to know what it was but I only hinted it was exceptionally awesome. "Where are you?" She texted. She told me she was on her way but that was quick if you ask me. I hastily made my way down the stairs where my eyes captured her beauty at first glance. There were others in the room much closer to me but I saw her first, it was just my reflexes I tried to convince myself.

As I made my way towards her I greeted her sisters and mom, then her. She smelt nice, she was pulchritudinous. She beckoned me to lead her to what I wanted to show her so badly so went and her expression said it all. I knew by the look on her face she loved it just as much as I did, if not more. When we got back downstairs, I watched her watching me as I pulled up my sweater sleeves as we sat together. I've always penchant the manner in which she sat; folding her legs. There's something about it that I found extremely attractive. She then folded her arms and playfully I followed as we laughed together. There we held hands and talk a little while as I enthralled her with my fluent words.

No sooner than the hands hit the digits 7 pm, the diapason began to enthrall our ears. It was song service time and the music chimed as if it was heavenly. We enjoyed the service very much, I for one thought that it was exhilarating.

As we walked together; her hand in mine and our hearts closely knit together in joy and elation. We had quite an interesting conversation while journeying home. When we got there I made it known unto her that I had something profounding to ask and eager she became. "What is it Nardo?" By then everyone was out of sight, they were walking ahead of us and we just stood there under the moonlight with its rays of crepuscular reflection looking down on us. I wasn't sure where to start. I know what I wanted to ask of her but still that wasn't the point, in fact it was neighbors with it; beside the point. "You are very special to me" I managed. "Nardo my family is waiting for me" she cut in, for she knew I was always a descriptive person to detail in expression. By then I tried my best to be laconic and I quickly said what I had to focusing my vision solely on her eyes, removing the red box of pure sterling silver jewel rings; engagement and wedding band. There in the moment I watched her eyes go in excitement and her pupils enlarged, if was something that usually happens whenever she looks at me. I just thought how pulchritude she was as I went down on one knee in the middle of the street. "Oh my, that's a ring!" She exclaimed. "Trace will you marry me?" I proposed. I could tell that her whole body was engaging in thrill mode and then it happened. "Yes!" She answered as I slipped the dazzling ring on her finger and bid her a good night.

CHAPTER SIX

On the eighth day of the same month we made our way to church, that bright and sunny Sabbath morning. Rays of sunshine scintillating on the verdure; lush green vegetation as I past them by. They reminded me of something, peace mayhap. I wondered what the plants would communicate to us had they been provided with the privilege of speaking for I'm very certain there is something to learn from them. I hastily made my way to the cab stop where I waited patiently for a cab to arrive, though I wanted to go already. Luckily for me, there came my church sister, honking me on to hop in.

"Happy Sabbath my dear brother Nardo and how are you doing this morning? It's so nice to see you." She proclaimed in excitement. "Happy Sabbath, I'm great thanks for asking and you?" "God is good." She replied. There was music playing on the inside, gospel music it was. With the windows wined all the way up, I could feel the air conditioner all over. When we arrived at church my first instinct was to look for Trace. "Did I reached first or had she?" was just the norm of a question that occasionally played on in my head. It was what we usually do. I made my way inside and sat. It was a wonderful service for the day. Our family band had won the trophy for Adventist youths. We both took photographs of it.

Trace went a few minutes early before it had ended with her family. As soon as it ended I journeyed on a quest to seek her. I walked on that street she usually does and I made my way to the supermarket that was shopped at more frequently but somehow I couldn't find her. I felt a sense of insularity taking over. It was at this point that I sent a message, however I had to succumb to the decision that it was time to head home. I went to the bus stop by the gas station where I mounted a cab and was well on my way home. There on I've received a call from her and though the decision was mine, not that she knew I was half way home. I've managed to head back into the town somehow as quickly as possible would allow. "The things we do for love" I thought.

It reminded me of Valentine's Day when I rushed in the town after having no success with retrieving a cab that soon in the morning. We hadn't prayed that evening. It had become a routine for us, one in which I intended to keep on going in good standing. We would occasionally pray together holding hands. The beginning of the week and the end of the week. By the time I catch up with Trace, she was well on her way home with the bags from the grocery store. I caught up to her just at the point where we usually depart and she was about to pray with me right there and then but mom beckoned that we did it at home. I was given a calendar of the year. It had a radio station on its cover so I showed it to mom and that was when she enquired on the day that it began the week. She then told me of an interim when Maria got one which begun on Monday and they had to throw it out.

It was at this point I thought how fortunate I was that mine started on the right day, it was a colorful calendar and I had a sense of philia about it. We got to the house. There I lay my feet in the pattern of Trace's, as we made our way down the steps. That night as we got to the house we prayed twice and something told me that the Lord's presence was amongst us, despite how undeserving we are. But that wasn't all; we were elated for the chance to talk. The thing is, I wasn't the type to just open up to everyone. I'm very selective of the few that I share my life and its problems that come along with it with. I've been through a whole lot in the past and I've actually considered suicide a few times.

I just couldn't get the grip on life's purpose so it'll be unfair to judge me on it. I've poured it all out to her, I don't know why but I really trusted her and I saw in her face a pair of listening eyes. They appeared to give off a pied reflection as the moon light gave its reflection just the same. We had quite the conversation from life on a whole to getting married and that was when she shared with me her deepest secret of a lifetime. It wasn't easy for her, the memory of it was fantod and she was afraid that I would leave her. This was when I held her hands as tears flowed down her cheeks and like a mirror I couldn't help but absorbed her emotions while at it. I didn't cry for I had to be strong for her but I was pretty sure we shared a slice of that cake equally amongst us. By means of reflexes, I wasted no time in drying her tears with the palm of my hands and fingers, "it's going to be okay, I'm not going anywhere. I'll always be with you." "No matter what?" "No matter what" I assured her.

It was then that we had our very first kiss. To say it was perfect would be degrading. It was blissful and enjoyably elegant.

We did again for proof of how awesome it was. Like a child I lifted her up and made way to go up the steps towards the gate but I stopped in my tracks and placed her on my leg to sit. There we cuddled and imagined watching the stars for counting and making a wish but the trees were present instead. Still that didn't take away from the marvelous time we were having.

   The next thing we know; it was getting late. It amazes me just how time adores dressing herself in the finest of linen so as to make her way on the fastest aircraft in history when two people are having a great time. We didn't want to depart but we knew we must; we needed to. In fact, we kept saying good night and bid our farewells with embracement but there we were just the same talking on and on. I must have come home though, for I found myself in my bed the following morning smiling as I thought of her and all that transpired last night.

   There was camp being held on Easter weekend and I've been invited but declined. The thing was, I planned on spending the holiday with you know who and that we did. I made her a Bitmoji that resembled her so perfectly and I thought she needed another to go along with, so she wouldn't be lonely so I made one that resembled me as well and how cute and adorable they were.

   Teacher's day was upon us and I had in mind to provide a gift that I see best fitting for the number one educator on planet earth; Princess Trace. As I contemplated on what to give, I finally decided to do what I do best, write a poem. It was entitled 'Princess Trace 2.0' and it states,

   "He sees magnificence in her soul,

   Just by looking in her eyes,

   And in a world where it seems so cold,

She lets him feel warmth inside.

Inside her arms,

He feels so safe,

Near or far,

He sees her face,

He sees magnificence within her soul...

He sees greatness waiting to be unfolded.

Happy teacher's day Trace."

I wrote it down and I was sure to accompany it with a pen as she will be writing her exams very soon so I saw it fit that a teacher should have a pen.

"It's a meaningful and thoughtful gift" I heard her smiled out the words from her mouth. That evening I went to Wednesday night prayer meeting, though Trace and her family hadn't. It was a rich service filled with some new information that presumed to be breathtaking. I learnt that God did not make us, only Adam and Eve because God does not deal with sin. Strange enough, I'm not sure what to believe but it was all from a book. When I told Trace about it, she was just as shocked as I was. "It does make sense though" she replied.

After the service, I've received a text message on my phone enquiring if I had brought the pen. Funny enough I said no, as a jest for I knew just how excited she was about it. It was drizzling liquid from the heavens above when I arrived at church but as soon as I was prepared to depart it advented to an abrupt cessation. Other than the strong petrichor emanating from the rapidly drying grass, there was not a trace of evidence that it had rained at all. When I arrived at her home she was most elated than ever before.

We kissed and cuddled all night long before bidding each other farewell. If we could have our own way, we'd stay up until morning together. "Thanks for those kind words Prince." She acknowledged me a few days later. Similar to Valentine's Day, she made me a poem also. It read:

"He is special though he does not see it,

He is gifted though he does not believe it,

He is all she needs though he at times questions it.

Maybe. Just maybe if you saw yourself the way I do.

Then maybe you'd realize that all those things are true.

I love you Prince Nardo.

ALWAYS AND FOREVER.

Let's do right by ourselves, each other but most importantly God.

Sweet dreams sweetie. We'll talk soon."

Just a day before mother's day we went to church. It was Sabbath. There was a program put in place especially for mothers by the women's ministry. To add, there was a preacher that preached at divine service; a savant of sound mind and elevation. It is of no hidden fact that when she opens her mouth, wisdom sprouts thereof. We were richly blessed that morning with the grace and loving kindness of our Lord and Saviour Jesus Christ.

In the afternoon for Adventist youths, they issued gifts for the mothers in the church. The following week was youth's day. I have been appointed with the task of personal ministries, though I knew what it was, I wasn't sure what it is that I am to do exactly. I dressed in the finest linen of jacket which gave off a dark grey tint of iridescent. When I arrived at church an elder assisted by explaining what it is and what to do and it was very straight forward so I became ready very yare. "Happy Sabbath ladies" I smiled at the girls. Trace helped me with the selection of the song so eagerly. In fact, she was elated to do it. While doing the personal ministries, I spotted the leader of the department looking on; well pleased. It was a wonderful day as I was happy to match dress code with her again. If we had a photograph together, it'll worth an infinite word for we are quite a pair, she and I, but we never did take any photos and neither did I walk her home that evening. She left before the service advanced to a cessation and I had watched her go with a prayer in my heart that she'll be safe on her way home. "I'm home" my phone said to me from Princess Trace and I smiled I'm response for I knew she was sure to know that. After all we were linked together always and forever.

CHAPTER SEVEN

It was getting tepid as the summer breeze was upon us. I could literally hear choirs of sound music outside my windows in the mornings as I get up to see the sunrise and thank the Lord for the twitter He sends each day. There was a reading camp that I had on my calendar. I wanted to participate in it so as to teach the young minds and groom them as to where they need to be. He thing is, I love literacy; reading and writing, more so I love to assist others. In fact, I recall assisting Trace with an assignment. We were to write a poem on global warming. The poem went something like this:

"It is said that green is life,
It is said that green is go,
It is said that red is hot,
It is said that red means stop.
But we cut down trees,
And we burn with ease,
And we see not that what we do displease,
The birds, the bees, nature as beautiful as these,
One day will soon never be,
For it is seldom less than unsightly.

Polluted air,
Illness for this generation and the ones to come,
Cut speed not and the world shall be done.
It is how miraculously it seems,
That the russet looking leaves on the earth walks swiftly to
meet the scintillating sunshine,
For that must be the reason indeed,
For the burning sensation when the leaves caress my feet.
When will we realize,
Just open our eyes,
For it is seldom less than unsightly,
Instead we complain how hot the sun is...
But whose fault is that?
God or Man?
Verily verily I say unto you,
That one man's garbage is another man's treasure,
Disposing bottles is what we do,
Why not save them to make use for the better?
It must have been a genius that came up with this idea,
For it blooms intellect in all its criteria,
Our reputation persuades us,
Likewise, our environment... dangerous.
People practically litter rubbish almost everywhere one can
think of,
For there's always a garbage somewhere in the blink of,
An eye, a sight, a vision, a scene,
It all seems foreign when the surroundings are clean.
Let us unite and join forces,
To stop deforestation and the burning of corpses.

With this I ask of you suavely,
Save a life with the assistance of alleviating global
warming.
Life is a cycle,
We should put in work; not idle,
And note this isn't a commandment from the Bible,
We must recycle.
Let's start by putting our garbage in its designated area,
Improper disposal leads to malaria,
Do right by the global warming; make it safer,
Let's unite, protect the ozone layer."

That seems to me an awesome poem or what I like to call it; a good read. I was well pleased with its outcome and especially elated that I've been presented with the opportunity to write it that I've entered it into a competition. Unfortunately, though, I never did get around to winning but it was never about winning. It was about love.

I attended a meeting which was held in Buck Bay where we discussed and planned the proceedings for the camp program in place. It was a great experience, meeting others, socializing and networking with potential and successful business personnel of reputable character. I've also taught English language and integrated science at a high school that summer. Being well rounded and on top of my game, I've successfully managed to showcase punctuality, respect and mannerism to each and every one.

I went to the beach with some of the teachers, staffs and friends there where I had a wonderful time, we played football on the sand; the men, as the ladies looked on and cheered. I could hear "Professor! Professor!" By numerous voices, though Ms. Moore overshadowed the others just the same. Professor became my new name. It was given by a Pastor at the school, he said that I walked like a professor and just started calling me that ever since. In fact, everyone picked up on it, and I meant everyone; literally. All staffs ranging from managerial positions right down, including the students. Sometimes I think they don't remember or know my birth name but who am I to complain, I don't mind it one bit, Professor it is. I scored a finisher after all my attempts; I guess I have aligned myself in the right place at the right time. Thereon we went for a swim; all of us.

Prior to entering the beach though, we were requested to pay a small admission but we never did get around to doing so. Perhaps we were v.i.ps or at least we made it certain that we were. It was two teacher's birthday and this was the celebration thereof. Prior to this day, mine had only just passed a few days before so it was three of us. The sun began to set it claws all over the heavens above, what a beautiful sight it was. As much as I would like to say we drove off into the sunset, we walked, well most of us did. It was close by, towards a restaurant but the cars couldn't drive themselves.

That was when we ordered a variety of meals, ranging from jerk chicken, steam fish, breadfruit, festival, plantain and so many others, including pepper. Yes, I said pepper but not just any pepper, this was country pepper which created quite a scene when I might have taken a bit too many. All in all, it was a marvelous day, I had loads of fun and I wish she was there.

I was sure to be early for work the following day. We usually have staff devotion in the staff room 15 minutes prior to class time and that on its own was enough to start the day well. One of the things about this educational institution is that worship is a key component, so as a result classes would begin before general assembly. "This is so that everyone will be present for devotion" I heard someone say. "Coming late isn't an excuse" I thought to myself.

That morning though, I've been asked to be the speaker and to choose the scripture reading that I will speak on, I accepted without hesitation. Upon listening to the introduction, I thought, is this me? But what I'm thankful for is that I know that there are some of us that took heed to the message presented unto them.

It was the season of school boy football and being the defending champion of the cup; we were preparing and practicing to reclaim the title again. There were days when I'd have class but went to match in support of the team, I must admit. The alternative would be having someone fill in for me until I return or briefly covering the aspect of the lesson with the students before I let them go home early. "We love Professor!" They'd often exclaim in joy. They were cooperative and very understanding so it was a win-win for everyone.

We drove to the match where the couch provided his motivational speech for the team and somehow it started to rain. I stood there as I watched the earth quickening her footsteps to meet the tears of the clouds in the heavens above. After which I glanced a coconut tree hovering above, it was doing quite a great job at keeping me dry. The thing is I had no umbrella, well not anymore at least. I had one but I loan it to someone and that was the cessation of it. Sometimes I miss the little umbrella but I'm sure she's doing fine or so I tell myself. Suddenly I recall that a coconut falling can be fatal to humans when contacting the cranium so I checked if there were coconuts at present.

It was then that the marvelous sun came making quite a scene so loud and boisterous that it was welcomed by everyone and the match began immediately thereafter. We won the finals as expected. It wasn't surprising at all. Our opponent had a big boy playing on their team and we were convinced he was overage for the league but it made no difference. The television company was there to capture it all on film and I drove Mrs. Moore's car.

It was closing on to examination time and it was time to invigilate exams. We all know the rule that a teacher can't invigilate exams for students that he or she teaches, but there was an exception. There was this big hall where classes would align themselves in their designated areas to sit exams so teacher's would assist other teachers if they weren't available. There was less work during this time. Between typing to printing papers, there weren't much to do. Crusade was upon us and I became a Bible instructor. Based on the agreement on my contract my time at the school was up but everyone wanted me to stay so I volunteered and did so.

I also became a member of the prayer band so I would now go to school in the mornings to invigilate exams, go out on the missionary field in the afternoons and attend crusade in the evenings. It was tiring but great.

I remember Trace telling me of a group work that she had at school and how much she disliked doing group works. "How so?" I asked. "No one does the work; it's usually left to one person." I quickly assumed that person was her. "But everyone says the same thing, so who are the persons that doesn't do the work?" I asked in a jocular tone, and we both laughed and smiled.

She had school the following day and a load of work to complete. I stayed up with her late until midnight to assist in completing it. We'd meet during the afternoons by the church; my Bible instructor colleagues and I, where we'd pray and have a worship session prior to visiting those that have indicated their interest in baptism. To say the day was lukewarm would be subtracting the impact that the sun was enforcing. We parked at a supermarket to pick up waters for the journey. "Oh happy day" I heard a voice say. The water went quickly; it must have been in a rush so I never did get around telling it to slow down. Yet, still the sun rages but incredibly enough the atmosphere was peaceful, it was cool and suddenly a wind approached us. It captivated our attention. It was then that we learnt the Holy Spirit is amongst us.

Houses upon houses did we visit and every person was worth the visit. I've realized that people are fighting with the urge to give their life into the Lord. They are holding onto something, something as little as to fix themselves first so that they won't sin when they do become converted but we worked on convincing with scriptures to prove that Jesus is the best way. There were many scriptures that we used over the period of time but the two that struck out to me the most was "Come now, and let us reason together, saith the Lord: though your sins be as scarlet, they shall be as white as snow; though they be red like crimson, they shall be as wool." Isaiah 1:18 KJV and "How long, ye simple ones, will ye love simplicity? And the scorners delight in their scorning, and fools hate knowledge?" Proverbs 1:22 KJV.

We beseech these individuals to come and accept the Lord, for how long shall they wait? I've seen elderly persons who's not ready to be baptized and I couldn't help but grew a sense of melancholy as a result.

CHAPTER EIGHT

The sky woke up with rays of sunshine on a peaceful heaven scent Sabbath morning. I got up quite early as I made my way into the proceedings of the great morning duties. Such as the like include, exercising and sunrise watching. Watching the sunrise has always been a key component. I couldn't leave it out, such immaculate beauty I just had to behold. I took it in all for myself, the thing was, the sunrise and I had quite the relationship going on; we were inseparable. When I pulled up at the church they were already issuing Bible study guides for the new quarter ahead. Unsurprisingly enough, Trace had them. I mean, of course she would. Why wouldn't she? I thought to myself.

"Hi..." "Hi..." We communicated. "Here's a quarterly" she said. 'I saved this one especially for you' I heard. We would often call them quarterly for they are meant to last for the quarter of the year then a new one would be issued. "Oh thanks but I've already received one from around the back" I used my most modest of voice possible. We could hear the announcements being presented as background noises but the loudest volume of them all was the electricity flowing between her and myself. She sat at a straight angle from me with me being in front. "So, tell me you'll be going to harvest" I flirted, knowing already she wasn't going. "No I'm not" she blushed. "Let me have a quarterly." "Nardo, you already have a quarterly." "For my sister" I beguiled. When I turn around, I could literally feel her blushing and whispers amongst her sisters, which might have been teasing and believe me when I say, I know teasing.

I was to participate in the harvest ingathering service so I made some preparations, after all I'm one who believes in being prepared at all times for action. At the harvest they would normally have just about all the ground provisions that one could possibly think of. Ironically enough my family and I was heading to the big city, the city where there's not enough ground provisions available for the taking. People there mostly purchase those type of things. The morning of the journey was cool and relaxing. We had a few things to do before we got on the bus that would take us there. I had a cheque to cash so there I stood in the bank as I observed my surroundings, I noticed how quite it was; a whisper is extremely loud and shouldn't be qualified as a whisper at all. I wasn't there for long. I got through quite quickly, or so I told myself.

It was hard felt sunny the moment we mounted the bus but were welcomed by some wet rain by another parish. We had to past that parish to get to the one we wanted to go initially. I thought of how great it would be to have Trace with us on the journey; I remember how fond she grew of the idea of us doing an all island road trip together, but just us. I messaged her the whole time as to keep her company for she was at home that day, until my battery died in the process and I had no other option but to reap what was left of the remains; thoughts on the day proceedings. We engaged into a whole conversation about assisting persons in need and I felt like she was only quoting what I would have said, yet it was so genuine.

We got to the city safe and sound with ample time for waiting in a big hall of some organization. I watched as I seated myself on a large comfy cushion-like chair. I counted the times the elevator went up as opposed to coming down and the sleek protocol in which was carried out by the front desk agent. At this time Trace was upset or not happy so I entered the patient mode and I waited. I must have doze off in the middle of it. "Nardo, let's go. Come on!" My brother said. So we were on the move again. The street was filled with mendicants at each corner. Some of them had a look of pity in their eyes but others appeared to be dangerous with a need of a pair of new jeans and a dialogue on not to walk where the bad dogs are. I mean their pants were a disaster; ripped with holes all over.

We went to Music Land where we picked up some strings for the guitar and there I saw a wide range of musical instruments and books on music of all sorts. It was beautiful, fine art at its purest form. Next up, we came upon book mart where I just wish I could take all the books there, would that I could. All in all, the day was great and so was the movie 'Spiderman' that we saw at the cinema. I made sure to grab something for Trace, I just had to. I saw it in a store and I thought of her instantly so I brought it back home for her. We got home very late though but I had a really great time.

I woke up to the good old gospel music playing in the background. It was the rise of the sun, the nascent of something great. The sky appeared diverse from its usual fashion, I guess it was due to the serotinal section of the year. She was already there waiting by the time I got to our meeting area. If I didn't know better, I'd say she was waiting for me. "For you" I handed over the gift which was perfectly wrapped and well put together. "Thank you." The day was filled with happiness, joy and much laughter as we played 'foot kicks' 'elbow nudging' and another which name is too much of a redamancy to mention. When I arrived at my abode I saw a text which said "I'll always be there for you, you can count on it. I had a wonderful time with you today. Thanks again for the gift, and for sitting with me. Continue to look to God and live for Him. Sweet dreams, good night Prince."

I had plans for beach with a few friends the following day. The rain made sure we didn't go, it just had to. But that never stroke as a bane to stop us from getting together. We decided to spend the day having a cookout just the same at the hotel. I've been chauffeured to the destination from home. It was only fitting; I mean being the noble gentle man of my caliber. It was quite a hill to reach the hotel but we made it somehow and words can't express enough just how much it was worth the journey. The view was immaculate; next to paradise.

I could see the whole town and it was cool there with beautiful lush green trees with fruits of all varieties. We played dominoes and I've realized just how great I was at it or perhaps that was due to the experience I've had of not winning a single game when playing with a certain man. It was as if he had x-ray vision to see through the blocks. The meals were delicious and so was the movie. We got home late that evening but it was a wonderful day.

Trace and I started a book club. We would usually read a book each week and at the end of the week, we would have the discussions thereof. It was an interesting way of bonding and though reading was always my thing, the very fact that she participated in doing it with me meant a whole lot. "I really enjoyed the conversations and reading Prince. I'd love to do it again soon. Thank you. God's will, the future. Good night." Then we hugged and went off to bed.

On Sabbath I watched as my mom and Trace had a conversation together. They were so pleasant, nice and cheerful to each other. "Hi, how are you?" Mom began. "Hi, I'm great thanks and you?" Trace responded. "Likewise. You don't speak much, do you?" "Not usually but when needs be." "Okay, I figured as much. I'm just as reserved as you are." "That's something we have in common." "What do you think of my son, Nardo?" "He is really awesome." "Okay, I'm okay with you both, all the best and say hi to your family for me." "Thank you, I'll do that." When I got home, I picked up the phone and I called Trace. "There are some things that have always been hard for me talking to people are one of them but it was never like that with you. I know that I'm not the easiest person to get along with but I truly admire your efforts. I had a really terrific day with you. The book club was awesome. I'm happy I did it and I'm happy I met you. You drive me crazy; sometimes knowing that I'd spend the day with you makes everything much easier." Trace expressed what she had on her mind. "I always knew that we connected in a way that only we could understand. We've got a bond like no other. Thanks. There isn't another I'd rather give my time and effort than you Princess. I had a wonderful day today, it was well spent. I can't wait to do it all over again. I don't regret having this book club with you. It has been a great experience. I'm happy I met you too." I responded thoughtfully.

Being President of the Rotaract club means doing the best I can to ensure that the society felt a sense of comfort and belonging. It meant that I had to undergo the necessary stages of leadership and lucky for me I know just who is the perfect example to follow; none other than Christ Jesus. I've been to a very important meeting, where I got the opportunity to network, meet and greet with other Presidents of diverse Rotary clubs. I was the youngest of the whole batch but that didn't take away from my offerings at the table.

I've learnt so much from these elderly folks. These are seasoned men and women who has the experience and knows a lot so I redeemed it a great privilege to have them in my presence. I listened keenly as they went up to make their speeches and I had to commend them for they were well deserving of their awards in which they've collected that day. Leaving that meeting to conduct a Bible study with a few guests was next on the agenda. I would occasionally make it to that appointment on time because of how important I prioritize it to be.

It's only such a tragedy to later learn that the lady had passed away. I know that people die all the time and that there is a better place than this earth but I felt a bit of melancholy taking over just the same. Trace and I have always had our share of ups and downs, good and bad but all in all, we never gave up. That night I heard her say the sweetest of things ever. "I don't even know where to start. I love that no matter how far we go we always find a way back to each other. I had a great time with you today. I knew I'd love the book you'd choose. You are truly an amazing, talented, kindhearted and remarkable human being and I'm lucky to have you in my life. Sweet dreams and good night Prince. Have fun in dreamland. May God continue to strengthen and use you to accomplish good things for yourself and others." I couldn't help but smile as I listened to the voice of an angel as I dozed off in dreamland.

CHAPTER NINE

The greatest day on earth has arrived once more; Sabbath. It was even more so great because we know it'll be spent together in happy harmony. I've made it my point of duty to be early that particular morning, as well as other mornings but this morning I was in for a race. It was only the greatest championship ever, to arrive at church before Trace did, plus I'd receive a trophy if I had. Believe me when I say, I had everything in place to make the task much easier but in reality I just happened to ran straight in her waiting for a hundred years until I arrive. "Unbelievable!" I thought. I knew she lived closer to the church than I did but I couldn't save the astonishment. "Ha! Hand it over" she made reference to her brand new trophy as I reached in my pocket and provided the same.

These trophies in which we spoke of time after time again were mere mythical belongings and as such a fragment of the imagination. Prior to today we went and made a list of five bulletins. Each items were to be things we intend on doing together. So we wrote them on separate papers, as curious as a cat to see what the other wrote so this became the day of divulgence. Time wined down to only a week until the Adventist laymen's Services and Industries prayer breakfast and as it announced I received a nudged on the arm lightly; titillate as I would pronounce it. I had a presentation to do at the prayer breakfast and this indicated just how much excited Trace grew in anticipation as the date got closer to the moment. As for the list we had, the exchange was sleek. Mine was pinned on me by a play of the palms and I gave mine shortly after while holding hands as we prayed. We never did look at them just yet though. We waited until it was time for us to have lunch. Before I opened the note though, I prayed. I don't know why I did, not that I need a reason to but I did. Slowly but surely the moment of truth came upon me as I count down the seconds. "5...4...3...2...for the love of Jesus Christ!" I slowly opened the note and observed the fluency of her font choice. It was written in ink by the hand and I could tell it was her penmanship for I knew it anywhere like the back of my hand.

As I read the words carefully I noted something systematically about each bullet. Just how much she wants us to spend time together and go on dates. As church was about to resume I saved seats for Maria and Trace, Marvette didn't return. As I was making my way to do the preliminaries, my android rang. "Princess Trace calling" it said. I didn't answer though for I saw and met her at the door. "Hi" we said all at once. "Where's Marvette? She won't be joining us?" "No, she'll be staying home. Where are the seats?" It was funny she asked. As I gave directions as to where they might have been, I wasn't convinced myself had I not known for sure and I could tell she felt the same. So I chauffeured them both to their seats. I felt like an usher in the process, either that or something equivalent to the perfect gentleman.

While I did the priliminaries, I was looking at everyone but overall all I saw was how beautiful of a smile a certain person gave me, which had the prodigious of effect on me. As a result, I begun smiling too, thanks to my team member Trace. "Could you help me with the opening hymn?" Maria asked in her kindest tone I'd imagined prior we went up together to lead out the preliminaries. "Sure." We each had an item to deliver as we waited around the back upon the appointed time. "Aren't you guys going to sit?" Trace sat. "I..." Maria made to say something but, "we are soldiers" I stepped in abruptly. "Okay sergeant major, suit yourself" she smiled in response.

It so happened that we waited a while so I went and got an extra chair so Maria could be seated. It was an extremely comfortable chair at that, I made sure of it with my touch. We then all sat together. Stomp! I felt on my feet, "not a soldier anymore?" Trace asked and somehow I could sense a kiss coming on but I remember she was one who is always agoraphobic so that one we swerved out but when we returned back inside I saw my books on my chair. "Trace must have placed them there" I thought, for saving the seats that they wouldn't be taken.

When we got home, I went through my Bible, I usually read this scripture before retiring for bed nightly; Romans 13:12-14 and to my surprised I met a note directed to me from you know who. As I read along, I could hear the sound of her voice and her expression as she called each words, and I could shell her scent just by thinking of her, a scent which reminded me of home.

The note said "I have yet another glorious day to record in my history. With you Prince I had another amazing day. I'm happy to say that it was so because I shared it with you Nardo. Thank you so much for being a part of mine and sharing yours with me Sweetie. I look forward to sharing another day with you. Good night and sweet dreams Prince. May God be with you. If I could I'd spend all the time in the world with you. You'll do great things. Don't you forget that; you're destined for greatness. May God continue to keep you Honey, remember His arms of love are always open to His children no matter how far from home they've wondered. I'll be your number one fan, not because it's a nice thing to do but because I genuinely believe in you Honey and if you ever need to be reminded of how great you are, you know how to reach me. I love your smile Sweetie." Sometimes words don't say enough, I thought to myself. All of this is the equivalent to say just how much she loves me dearly.

The big day has arrived or shall I say the big night. I had quite the presentation to go with as I've selected the topic 'faith.' It was an all-night prayer fasting which went from 10 PM to 5 AM. I didn't sleep at all. It was way too interesting for one to nap. The night had its sure way of creeping as it went along but before you know it, it was morning. I've been introduced in the sweetest and most charming way I have ever been before.

As my introductory speaker continued, I wondered if I was the one she spoke of. She had asked me what I'd like to become earlier that day and it fitted in perfectly in her introduction, though I never did know her reason for enquiring... until now.

My presentation was spicy and not too long if I might add. Better spicy and end on a high than long and drawn out I always say. I went on and on about this man and a breadfruit tree. "We talk so much of faith from time to time but do we really know what it means to have faith? What is faith exactly? The question I would like to put forth, one might say it is to believe but according to English language, believing is a verb and faith is the noun to that same verb. Therefore, they mean the same thing. Hence, to say to have faith is to believe is saying to have faith is to have faith. We just can't use a word to define itself, now can we? We can then turn to the Bible where it states that faith is the substance of things hoped for, the evidence of things not seen. Hebrews 11:1 KJV but what does this entire statement means? There was a certain man who was afraid of heights; he was acrophobic.

But he needed to pick a breadfruit from a tree that was multiple times taller than he was. But he was confident that he could retrieve the fruits without falling and he would be safe, not because he was such a great and skilled man at climbing but because of his faith that he placed in God to see him through. It so came to past that he did pick the breadfruits and he did remain safe. The point is people, had he placed his faith in falling, he would in turn reap the benefits thereof but he placed his faith in the true and living God and as such he got the reward. Likewise, we are to have strong faith in God in order to come out victorious even when the odds are against us. I thank you, may God bless you abundantly."

I knew that the people got the message then because they all made sure everyone heard their amen, even those out on the street. The rest of the night was incredibly awesome and filled with more informative presentations and a great deal of praying.

As the dawn approached her feet closer towards us, we went upstairs for refreshments.

It was then via means of socializing that I've learnt a funeral would be held in the afternoon. I'm not one for funerals though, I never did get around to liking them very much so I went home to get some rest. Funny enough it didn't come immediately but when it did, it really did.

The following week I went to a work day by the church. Our church building is under construction so they'd occasionally request assistance by the members as best as possible. So I volunteered my services willingly. We spent the day moving a vast amount of materials closer so they will be of an easier access when needed. I also went in the kitchen, my favourite part. Then I helped the ladies move some stuffs in the vespers room. The day was incredible. I really do enjoy working with these men.

When I got home I called Trace, to let her know I was great and to wish her a good night. I decided to give her a bedtime story by means of tucking her in. I had no idea what to say though but the words just came one after the other.

"Once upon a time, a beautiful lady and a handsome gentleman began their day with work and a busy schedule. However, they finally got the time and began to make it count. Every second mattered, they didn't waste any. It didn't matter that they had forever together. Every second was precious. So they got closer and closer and had a very important question to ask each other...to be continued. Goodnight my lady, you are royalty. Sweet dreams and I hope you remember God." "Not fair! I so want to hear more, why did you end it there? I'll wait to hear it though. Good night sir. Sweet dreams, may God watch over you and your family."

CHAPTER TEN

The air felt pleasant and nurturing as the sun came out quite beautiful as it usually does. I got up early and went on my morning exercise routine. There was something different about this morning. The sun came out later than yesterday. It would appear that the summer has finally advanced to a cessation, just when we had started having a good time.

September morning and the season of school begin. I've only just got accepted into college and it was quite the most extravagant of feeling, I must admit. There I enrolled in the study of becoming an educator. One that is of noble character and will make the best of what he has been provided with to do great things.

The truth of the matter is Trace too had school. I can recall her being sorry for so many things, apologizing for one thing or the other and me listening and accepting these apologies as they were coming from a sincere place. I believe in fairness. I know that we aren't perfect but what matters is that we do our best, even if our best outdoes us most of the time. I too am sorry for not being able to spend as much time with her as I would hope to. I never did get around to telling her that I would be off to camp in accurate detail. Beats me, I hadn't known myself. But sometimes some things are just beyond our control.

The journey was long. The can be described as scorching, yet excitingly tiresome I'm amazed to declare. We had to past numerous of cities to get to the camp and judging by our driving, one would think we aren't sure exactly where we are heading. Lucky enough for us we were blessed with directions from the Lord's messenger unto us. By the time we got to the destination, it was well into Sabbath day. So I went to prepare myself for worship service which was very informative and educational. I really like the effort and conviction in which the speaker puts forth to connect to us the audience. In fact, he wrote a book about it and I intend on reading it.

Everyone was so friendly and kind; welcoming and warm. It was so easy to meet new friends and join in a fellowship that is lasting. In waking up come the dawn, it was like mother's cooking in the kitchen smelling up that sweet savour as the sun stretched his fingers to touch my face.

I woke up. Preaching, the reading of scripture, singing and laughter could be overheard as the men of my dorm engaged in their morning worship sessions. This I imagined to be such a great way to begin the day. I think I took longer than the usual to get dressed for service though. Mayhap because of only walking a few feet away. For the Bible study, we went on a tour of historical sites on the campus. There we made several stops at particular areas and witnessed what each area meant. We climbed hills and valleys, rivers and lakes, path bushes and thought of the day when God would return; at the very least I sure did.

There was a speaker for the evening program that made her mark and I really appreciate all that she's said. I had a great deal of making the level of melancholy in mankind next to demolish; I believe people call it fun as a short version. That night I stayed up late, knowing tomorrow I'd be heading back home where I could sleep in my nice and comfortable bed. Yet, when the dawn arrived I woke up early just the same. How I did it is still a mystery to me.

When I got home I was thankful for I knew that God was watching over me. "Will you watch the sunrise with me?" I had made my request known unto her. "Yes I'd love to." So we began anticipating that Tuesday morning so we could do so. "The sooner we go to bed; the sooner the morning will arrive." That proved to be true, I thereon found myself agreeing with her.

That morning was a very special morning so we woke up quite early. "Hi, did you make up for the sleep you've lost?" She asked. "Yes I did." "That's even better. Let's watch the sunrise Honey." Okay what does it look like to you?" "little streaks of red behind some dark clouds. How about you?" "It's beautiful. This is nice." "Yes it is." "Thanks for watching with me. Ecclesiastes 11:7." "Okay, you're welcome Honey, I should have a long time ago. I'm sorry I didn't. Interesting scripture." "I'm just happy you did now Honey, the past cannot be changed. We can only make the best of the present which will determine the future so apology accepted. Yes, I meant to share that scripture with you at a moment like this. I hope your day will be fantastic. I hope it has started on a great note and will continue to strike up that octave. May God be with you and keep you safe always." "This is a perfect day for us Nardo."

Now as promised I took her home on a random afternoon. It wasn't planned, but it happened. Occasionally I'd partake in doing so from ever since. It became a part of my duty: highly expected of me. The thing about this though was that it would often take her two to three hours to arrive from school on the bus to the point where I'd meet her and bring her home. Patiently I waited as if it was high priority of mine; just as she's important. Sometimes it would rain. We liked the rain.

On one particular evening we had quite the scene with her umbrella. Though we didn't mind getting wet together. In our hometown its quite the most difficult of tasks to predict the weather; one minute nice and sunny, the other extra nice and rainy. So I got her a hand fan from one of those stores. I saw it and I thought it would be nice and may come in handy. Though I never did see her use it, she extremely elated about it and appreciated it very much. With only five minutes to head back to school after dropping her home, I made it in time. I usually do. "A lot can happen in five minutes" a wise man often says. Sometimes we would take rides on an extravagant roller coaster. We'd go up so high we feel like we can touch the stars and so low we feel like we have our heads stuck under the earth with no clouds to hydrate us from the cataclysm of a tragic catastrophe. But that never became a bane to us from fastening our seatbelts. After all, safety first. So her knight and shining armour I am.

Like an augury I know her reason for fear of being alone, especially on the road so I was always there she could always rest assure. Even on evening from church where we'd just have communion. There ran into each other at the supermarket. Eyes flusters as they met like the summer meets the tourist at the beaches in Jamaica. She was always a nervous one, especially when in my presence. There I brought the groceries as we had quite the conversation on the day in church and her mom was just happy to see me that evening. From taking the challenge of reaching church before the other, only to end up arriving at the same time to deciding who'd get that trophy. We probably should have a trophy for taking trips together, though we'd planned on it, which was forth-coming. Going on trips had always been a thing of enjoying as there came up a school trip for Trace but it had a casual dress code to the requirements. So I went and prepared a rubric to grade her.

I've never seen her in jean and sneaker before as this would be the very first time. I graded for neatness, how much she resembles Trace, outfit pairing and beauty. Believe me when I say, she nailed it. Not just with an ordinary hammer but a prodigious sledge hammer built for Thor. "That's quite a list you've got there." "Yes and I can't wait to mark it." "Of that I'm sure." "Just as I'm sure you can't wait to be examined." "I'm not a fan of test. They make me nervous." "What if I told you that this test is diverse to any other?" "It doesn't make it any easier for me." "You're a natural. You have nothing to worry about, especially when it's been marked by Professor." "If you say so. Be careful Professor, other students might get jealous." "They'll understand that you come first." "I don't think they will." "I guess I'll have to include that into their lesson." "That just might work." "Okay that's the plan." "For you" she handed me a snack. "You said you liked nuts, right?" That was very thoughtful I thought and it made me feel like she genuinely cares for remembering details such as these.

Sometimes I think of the future. Oh what it has in store for us. Will I live until I'm a hundred-year-old? Will people be able to speak good things at my funeral? Or am I a bad person? In day dreaming with these subconscious thoughts I get interrupted by the slightest of things. It's the simplest of things that gets me started sometimes and I have a way of going on and on about how great things are. Even when reality has its way of declaring otherwise.

But that never stopped me from having hope, from having faith that there is still much to be thankful for. I have life and I have God; I have everything. 'If God is all you have, you have all you need.' Someone of a reputable character once informed me and me being me, I took to those words. I recite them from time to time, on a daily basis.

Day in and day out I try my utmost best to be the best individual I can possibly be. Only falling short as my best never turns out so well. It's not true what they say after all. Our best aren't always good enough. So as I walk this street of suicide, not knowing I'm heading for my doom. That my end is waiting on me around the corner.

Had I known, would I have swerved and head back? I think not. I wouldn't have it any other way. Intoxicated with mythical elements of what the world defines as love I decided to write her a letter. If she can read this, then it means that I've finally worked up the courage of mailing it. The curtains are closing now. It's time to wash out the dye from my hair and hang up the golden shoes I've ran this marathon with. It's been quite the journey. Now the fans no longer love me. So it's getting darker...I'm losing vision and the waves are coming in...

"In a different light,
In a different moment,
In a different instant,
In a different world.
In a different atmosphere,
In a different legacy,
In a different location,
In a different perpetual second.
We could have been together,
We could have made life together,
But some things...some things just aren't meant to last forever.
So in a different life, I will meet you there.
So farewell my love, and take care."
It's quite a thing to live in the world of imagination,
A world where there's perpetual occurrences and illusions,
Let's be frank really quick and get one thing straight,
If I will but wait, someday I will awake.
To have patience is to have endurance,
To have tolerance but not the lack of assurance,
I imagine what it would be like to live in a real world,
A world where there's an ice box where my heart used to be,
A world where I'm suffocating with fears,
A world where I'm a tear drop in an ocean full of flames,
A world where I gave my all in pain.
But that isn't the worst part,
Pain I can handle,
It's the suffering that comes along with,

After realising it was all for nothing.
So catch that grenade I did,
Now I'm stuck with the illusion of how well it could have been.
I imagine what it would be like to live in a real world,
But I know that for a dead man that'll never be.

END
Thank you for reading.